THE ANIMALS'
CHRISTMAS
CAROL

FOR JILL & COLIN

A TEMPLAR BOOK

PUBLISHED IN THE UNITED STATES IN 2001 BY THE MILLBROOK PRESS, INC.
2 OLD NEW MILFORD ROAD, BROOKFIELD, CT. 06804

PUBLISHED SIMULTANEOUSLY IN GREAT BRITAIN BY THE TEMPLAR COMPANY PLC
PIPPBROOK MILL, LONDON ROAD, DORKING, SURREY RH4 1JE, GREAT BRITAIN

DESIGNED BY MIKE JOLLEY

LIBRARY OF CONGRESS CATALOGING-IN-PUBLICATION DATA

WARD, HELEN, 1962-
THE ANIMALS' CHRISTMAS CAROL / HELEN WARD.
P. CM.
"A TEMPLAR BOOK"—COPR. P.
SUMMARY: MANY DIFFERENT ANIMALS COME TO BESTOW THEIR OWN SPECIAL GIFTS ON THE NEWBORN CHRIST CHILD.
ISBN 0-7613-2408-9 (LIB. BDG.) — ISBN 0-7613-1496-2 (TRADE)
1. JESUS CHRIST—NATIVITY—JUVENILE FICTION. [1. JESUS CHRIST—NATIVITY—FICTION.
2. ANIMALS—FICTION. 3. STORIES IN RHYME.] I. TITLE.

PZ8.3.W2133 AN 2001
[E]—DC21   2001030058

PRINTED IN BELGIUM BY PROOST

THE ANIMALS' CHRISTMAS CAROL

HELEN WARD

THE MILLBROOK PRESS
BROOKFIELD, CONNECTICUT

IN A DARKENING SKY

a star shone bright,

Over Bethlehem *one winter's night.*

Over the roofs of the sleeping town,

On a humble stable

the star shone down.

FOR A CHILD WAS BORN

that holy night,

And there within the candlelight,

While warm and safe the people sleep,

The animals a vigil keep.

As the newborn child in the manger slept

The creatures all around him crept,

And though he woke he did not cry

As they sang their
gentle lullaby...

"I," SAID THE DOG,

all black and white,

"I brought the sheep down from the hill tonight,

So the shepherds might *follow*

your shining light.

I," said the dog,

all black and white.

"WE,"

said the cow

and her calf, white and red,

"We gave up our manger for your bed,

And our soft sweet hay

to pillow your head.

We," said the cow

and her calf, white and red.

"We," said the lion
and the old brown bear,

"Will stand guard outside in the cold night air

To gently growl at the **shadows**

that dare come too close,"

said the lion and bear.

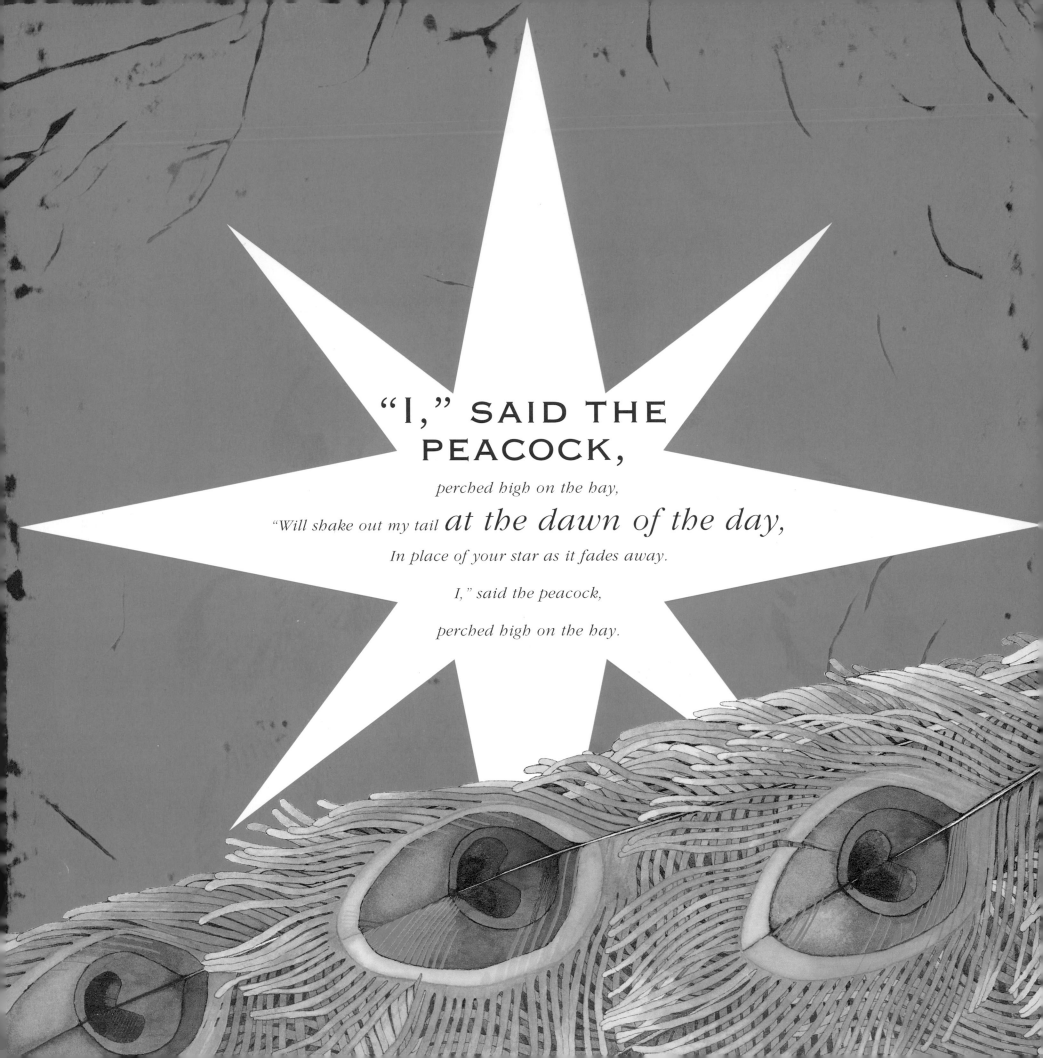

"I," SAID THE
PEACOCK,

perched high on the hay,

"Will shake out my tail at the dawn of the day,

In place of your star as it fades away.

I," said the peacock,

perched high on the hay.

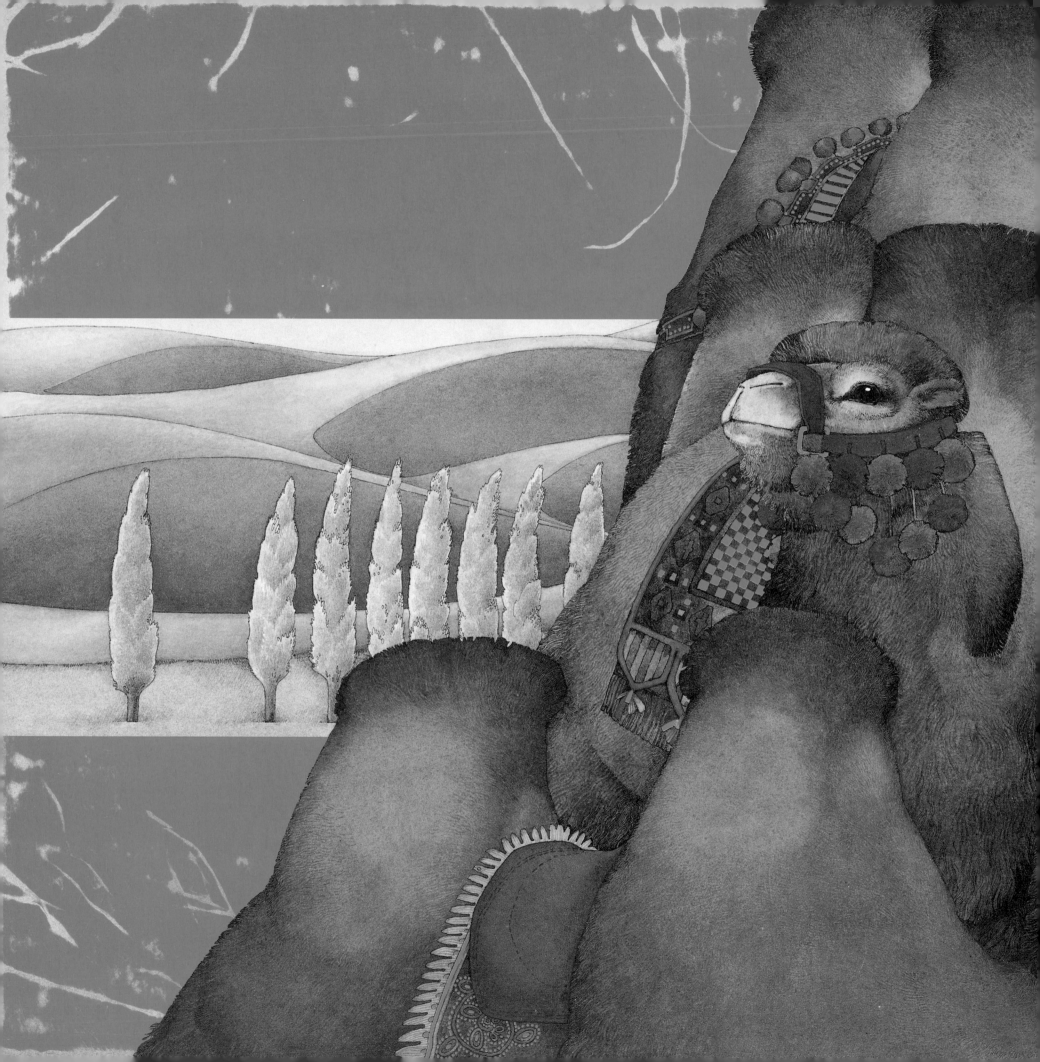

"WE," SAID THE CAMELS

from Eastern lands,

"We carried three men over desert sands

To place their *gifts in your tiny hands.*

We," said the camels

from Eastern lands.

THE BEES BUZZED,

"There is no gift sweeter than ours –

The best of the summer collected from flowers,

And beeswax for candles

to light the dark hours."

The bees buzzed, "No gift will
shine brighter than ours."

THE MOTH SAID,

"This candle flame
steady will stay.

Though I'm drawn to the light

I will stay away."

Said the spider, " I'll spin a fine web while you lay

To keep the small biters and stingers away."

"I," SAID THE MONGOOSE,

grizzled and gray,

"Will keep all the poisonous snakes at bay,

Will nip and snap 'til they slide away,

But *I'll keep watch* still,"

said the mongoose gray.

"OUR RESTFUL SONG,"

said the turtledove,

"We'll coo from the rafters up above."

"Coo," *sang the dove.*

"Duroo!" *sang his love.*

"We give you our song,"

sang the turtledove.

"I," SAID THE RAM

with the curly horn,

"I give my wool
to keep you warm,

Made into a blanket for Christmas morn.

I," said the ram

with the curly horn.

"I," SAID THE ROOSTER,

"Was so fine and loud,

That every hen in the inn-yard bowed.

But on this quiet morning,

I'll be less proud.

I will keep the peace,

and not crow too loud."

"I," SAID THE
WOODWORM,

humble and small,

"Can barely give
any gift at all,

But to spare the oak of your precious stall.

I," said the woodworm,

humble and small.

THE DONKEY dipped his sleepy head

And listened to all that the animals said,

As into the stable slipped *a glimmer of dawn.*

"I," sang the donkey, tired and worn,

"I traveled surefooted uphill and down

To bring your mother to Bethlehem town,

To this humble stable where you were born

To sleep safe in the hay on

Christmas morn."

So the beasts

with hooves and paws and wings,

And all the little creeping things,

Filled the stable,

warm and bright,

with love and peace

that Christmas night.

Helen Ward's

THE ANIMALS'
CHRISTMAS CAROL

Down through the ages children have sung carols as part of the celebration of Christmas. Through their familiar words and music such melodies help conjure, year after year, the image of the traditional nativity—Mary, Joseph, the shepherds, and the wise men, all gathered in the dark stable around the Baby Jesus. But what nativity scene would be complete without the traditional animals in attendance too—the oxen lowing in their stalls, the sheep fresh down from the hills, and the faithful donkey still watching over his precious burden? So it is little wonder that animals have their special place in the history of Christmas music. The visiting creatures sometimes change according to country and belief, but more often than not they also come bearing gifts for the newborn Savior.

In conceiving her own version of such a carol, Ward took inspiration from "The Friendly Beasts," a traditional song with a history that goes back many hundreds of years. Little is known about the origins of the text, but the tune is based on a medieval French melody called "Orientis Partibus." Written in the late twelfth or early thirteenth century by Pierre de Corbeil, the melody was originally associated with a Christmas text that began "Orientis partibus adventavis asinus," or "From the Eastern lands the donkey is now come."

The words and music for "The Friendly Beasts" are printed opposite, but for her version Ward wanted to add verses sung by myriad creatures, from the exotic peacock to the humble woodworm, all come to bring their own special gift to the Christ Child, no matter how small, united as they are by the true spirit of Christmas giving.

Jesus our bro-ther, kind and good, Was hum-bly born in a sta-ble rude; And the

friend—ly beasts a—round Him stood, Je—sus our broth—er, kind and good.

"I," said the donkey, shaggy and brown,
"I carried His mother uphill and down;
I carried her safely to Bethlehem town.
I," said the donkey, shaggy and brown.

"I," said the sheep with curly horn,
"I gave Him my wool for a blanket warm,
He wore my coat on Christmas morn.
I," said the sheep with curly horn.

"I," said the cow, all white and red,
"I gave Him my manger for His bed;
I gave Him my hay to pillow His head.
I," said the cow, all white and red.

"I," said the dove, from the rafters high,
"I cooed Him to sleep so He would not cry,
We cooed Him to sleep, my mate and I.
I," said the dove from the rafters high.

And every beast, by some good spell,
In the stable dark was glad to tell
Of the gift they gave Emmanuel,
The gift they gave Emmanuel.